Cheese Louise

written by David Michael Slater

illustrated by Steve Cowden

WALRUS
BOOKS

To Zach, Molly, Naava, Julia, Audrey, Ryan and Ross

For additional information, please contact Whitecap Books,
351 Lynn Avenue, North Vancouver, BC V7J 2C4.

Edited by Allison Haupt
Proofread by Elizabeth McLean
Cover and interior design by Michela Sorrentino

Printed and bound in China.

Library and Archives Canada Cataloguing in Publication
Slater, David Michael
Cheese Louise / written by David Michael Slater; illustrated by Steve Cowden.
ISBN 1-55285-721-2
I. Cowden, Steve II. Title.
PZ7.S62887Ch 2005   j813'.54   C2005-901922-0

The publisher acknowledges the support of the Canada Council for the Arts
and the Cultural Services Branch of the Government of British Columbia for our publishing program.
We acknowledge the financial support of the Government of Canada through the
Book Industry Development Program for our publishing activities.

WHAM!

Something shook Louise awake. She poked her head into the fresh air of the refrigerator. A carrot and a chubby ear of corn looked at her from the back of the drawer.

"Hi, I'm Cheese Louise,"

she whispered.

"Where am I?"

"You're obviously not a cheese *whiz*," the carrot chuckled.

"This Cheese Louise has holes in her head," he added.

"All *Swiss* cheeses have holes in their heads!"

said the corn. "Don't mind him, Louise. You're in the bottom drawer. I'm Pop Corn, and this is Seymour Carrot. Welcome to the Wait."

"What's the Wait?" asked Louise, feeling foolish.

"Didn't they teach you *anything* at the supermarket?" cried the carrot.

"Don't be so sour, Seymour. She's fresh from the factory." Pop Corn wrapped his husk around Louise. "Let me explain," he said, leading her up a shelf.

"We're all waiting to be chosen," Pop Corn said.

"Yeah, so we don't go to waste," added Seymour Carrot.
"There's nothing worse than getting moldy!

So try to look your best when the lights come on."

Louise was thinking nervously about all this when

WHAM!

everything shook again. "What was that?" Louise asked.
Pop Corn sighed. "Stand back and you'll see. The door is a
little loose."

TOMATO
KETCHUP

WHAM!

Something hit the fridge door, the latch clicked, and the door popped open, just for a moment.

WHAM!

It happened again, but this time the door opened enough for a hideous paw to snake through the crack. But the door was heavy. The paw vanished just before it swung shut.

"That was Kit," warned Pop Corn, "the nastiest cat ever to prowl a linoleum floor. He's always trying to get into the refrigerator."

"And if he grabs you," added Seymour, "he'll just roll you around on the floor until someone has to throw you away.

You'd be wasted!"

"Just last week," Pop Corn said with a shiver, "he almost snatched a turkey club sandwich from the second shelf. The brave little lunch would have been a goner if he hadn't poked Kit in the eye with his toothpick."

"So, Cheesy,"

Seymour Carrot said, "if you keep away from Kit, someday you might be chosen." Slipping back into the bottom drawer, he added, "Even if you've got holes in your head!"

Pop Corn smiled at Louise. "Ignore that cantankerous carrot," he said. "You'll be chosen soon enough." He turned and jumped down, pulling the drawer closed behind him.

A bright light shone down on the shelf. Louise tried to stand still as a giant hand reached over her and into a bread bag. **"Hooray! Hooray!"** she heard the little slice call as it was carried away. **"I'm toast!"** The refrigerator door swung shut, and the bright light was gone.

Louise slunk into a corner and slumped against the shelf. "How will I ever be chosen with these horrible holes?" she whimpered.

Louise looked around and noticed she was sitting next to a rather hefty bowl of chocolate pudding.

"You poor cheese," he sighed. "I can see right through you! You want to hide those holes, don't you? Am I right? With chocolate, maybe?" Louise considered the pudding's suggestion for a moment, then her eyes lit up with hope. "I thought so!" he cried. "Go on and help yourself—the proof is in the pudding. By the way, you can call me Moose."

Cheese Louise filled herself up with chocolate pudding and lay down on the middle of the shelf. "No one can see through me now," she thought to herself.

"I'm perfect."

Soon, the bright light shone again. Louise opened one eye as the giant hand hovered above her.

"Choose me. Choose me," she whispered. But the hand moved past her and picked up a piece of pie. Louise could see the little cherries grinning as the plate passed above her.

Suddenly,

there was a great gasp from the others in the refrigerator. The hand paused on its way out, and Louise looked through the open door. Barreling toward the shelves, at full speed, was **Kit the Cat!**

He was the meanest, scariest-looking beast she could imagine. He had sharp gray and white whiskers and a black patch over his left eye. His good eye was yellow and deep and truly terrifying. Cheese Louise held her breath. Kit made a snarling leap toward her shelf, but the door slammed shut just in time!

A great THUD

shook the refrigerator, and everyone inside heaved a huge sigh of relief.

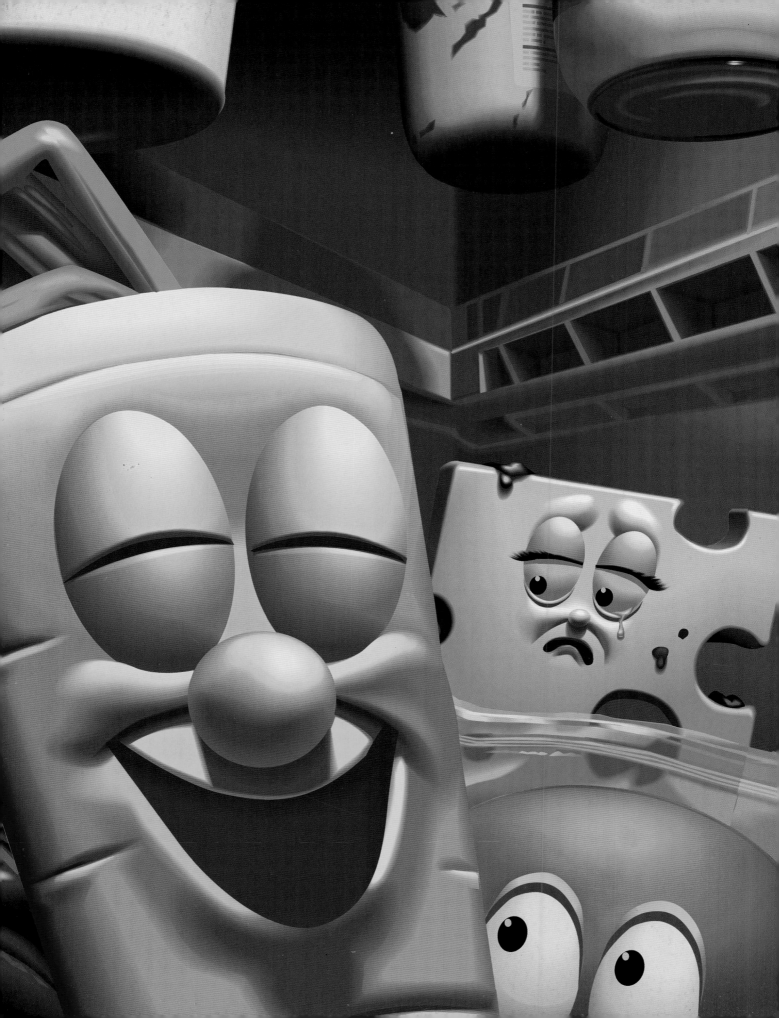

Frightened and sad, Louise cleaned herself off and slipped back down to the bottom drawer. She wanted to curl up inside her bag forever. When Seymour Carrot saw her with tiny bits of chocolate pudding still clinging to her edges, he began to laugh. "Hey Pop," he howled, "here's a sight for sore ears!"

"Oh, leave her alone, you tapering root!" snapped Pop Corn. He was about to say something else when the refrigerator lights began flashing on and off. "It's the emergency alarm," Pop Corn exclaimed. "The Leader has called a meeting.

Let's go! Let's go! Move it, foodstuffs!"

Cheese Louise followed Pop Corn, Seymour Carrot and all the others up the shelves of the refrigerator.

Soon, everyone was
packed

together on the top shelf. In front of
the crowd stood a wise-looking box of
baking soda. "Is that the Leader?"
whispered Louise.

"Of course," replied Seymour Carrot.

"Some say she's as old as the refrigerator, but no one knows for sure. Now shush."

Their Leader cleared her throat.

"We have an emergency," she said in a scratchy voice. "It is past bedtime, and our lookouts have spotted a yogurt named Humphrey stranded on the table." Everyone gasped. The Leader continued, "Humphrey is too frightened to climb down. If Kit doesn't get him first, he'll spoil overnight! We need a brave volunteer who can plug Kit's nose so the rescue team can get to Humphrey."

"He won't wake up if he can't smell anything," explained Pop Corn. "But who could get close enough to do it? He still has one good eye, and he's smart.

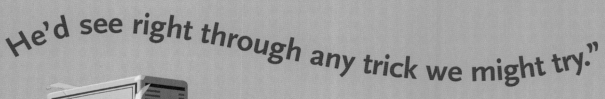
He'd see right through any trick we might try."

That gave Louise an idea.
She stood up tall and declared,

"I can do it!"

An enthusiastic cheer went around for Cheese Louise. The Leader called her over, and Louise whispered the plan to her.

"Fabulous," proclaimed the Leader. "What a brave cheese you are. We must act quickly.

To the door!" she cried. Everyone followed her to the edge of the bottom shelf. It took all their strength to push open the huge door from the inside.

Cheese Louise stepped timidly out onto the cool kitchen floor carrying a bag clip given to her by a sack of tortillas. She trembled as she looked at Kit sleeping on his pillow next to the table. Cheese Louise sneaked toward Kit. She could hear him growling in his sleep as she crept closer and closer and closer.

Finally,

Louise stood within reach of Kit's nose. She leaned forward slowly, clutching the bag clip.

Kit began to **twitch.** His nose moved from side to side; his eye was beginning to open! Louise was quaking with fear, but she was running out of time. She took one last deep breath, leaned over so her biggest hole was right in front of Kit's good eye and —

POP!

—put the bag clip on Kit's nose.

Kit's yellow eye snapped open in surprise,
but it stared right through Louise! He growled and blinked while Louise held perfectly still. Kit looked and looked, but nothing seemed out of the ordinary. He snarled and yawned, then closed his eye again and started to snore.

The rescue team slipped silently out of the refrigerator. They made a safety net of cling wrap for Humphrey, and he jumped down into it from the table.

When the team had Humphrey safely back inside the fridge, Louise removed the clip from Kit's nose and hurried back to the door, where she was greeted with cheers.

Cheese Louise was a hero!

When Louise climbed back inside, Humphrey said "If it weren't for you, I'd be in the disposal by now. Thank you from the bottom of my container."

Louise didn't think she could ever be happier.

But she was wrong.

Suddenly, the bright light shone down. Everyone became quiet and still. Pop Corn and Seymour Carrot were next to Louise; they were both grinning.

"Look! Look!" they whispered excitedly. Louise peeked up, and there it was: a huge hand right over her head. She held her breath as giant fingers reached out and carefully lifted her into the air.

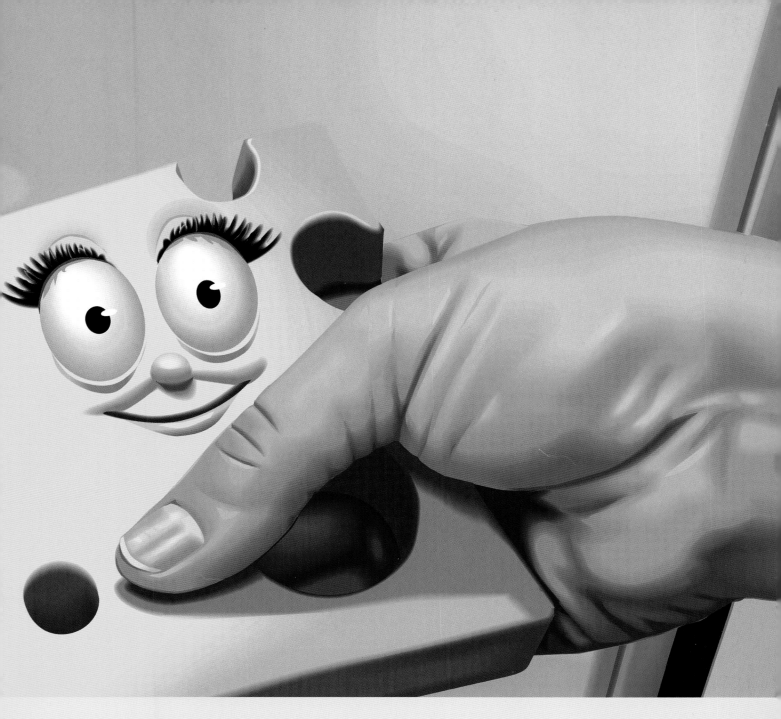

"Good bye, darling!" shouted Pop Corn, waving his husk.
"No one will ever forget you!"

"Ciao, Cheesy!" laughed Seymour Carrot. Humphrey blew her a kiss.

"Here's looking through you, kid!" he called.

Louise
smiled down at her friends as she was carried away. The best part of
being chosen was knowing that all the Swiss cheeses who
came to the fridge in the future would hear her story and be
proud to be just like her, the famous Cheese Louise.

THE END